The Lost Happy Endings

Carol Ann Duffy
&
Jane Ray

BLOOMSBURY
CHILDREN'S
BOOKS

Jub's job was important and she was very proud of it. Each evening when dusk was removing the outline of things, like a rubber, Jub had to shoulder her big green sack and carry all the Happy Endings of stories from one end of the forest to the other in time for everybody's bedtime. Once she had reached the edge of the forest, Jub had to climb to the top of a huge old oak tree, still with her sack on her back, and sit on the tallest branch.

Then, very carefully, Jub would open the sack and shake out the Happy Endings into the violet evening air. She was good at this because she had six fingers on each small hand.

went

the very end

and because she loved and they happy

fell in love him so very much

happily ever after

For Ella, Vivien, Rosie and Annie with love
C.A.D.

In memory of my mother, Barbara
J.R.

First published in Great Britain in 2006 by Bloomsbury Publishing Plc,
36 Soho Square, London, W1D 3QY

A CIP catalogue record of this book is available from the British Library

ISBN 978 0 7475 7922 9

Printed in Belgium by Proost

10 9 8 7 6 5 4 3 2

All papers used by Bloomsbury Publishing are natural, recyclable products made from
wood grown in well-managed forests. The manufacturing processes conform to the environmental
regulations of the country of origin.

Some of the Endings drifted away like breath and others fluttered upwards like moths fumbling for light. Some looked like fireflies disappearing among the kindling of the leaves and twigs and some were fireworks, zipping skywards like rockets and flouncing off in a jackpot of sparks high above the forest.

When the last Ending was out of the sack, Jub would scamper and rustle her way down to the ground and set off homewards through the darkening woods. Sometimes the eyes of owls flashed from the trees like torches and made her jump, or bats skimmed the top of her head like living frisbees and she squeaked with alarm, but Jub trotted quickly along and was soon home in her own cosy hole.

and they all lived happily ever after...

She would sleep quite late the following day. By the time she'd shopped, cooked, laundered, ironed, read a bit of her new book and perhaps visited a neighbour in another hole, the Happy Endings had flown back to the forest like homing pigeons and were hanging from the ancient silver birch all ready for Jub to collect once again.

One evening, as Jub set off with her full sack, she noticed scarves of mist draped in the trees. One of them noosed itself round Jub's neck, soft and damp, and made her shiver.

By the time she had reached the middle of the forest the mist had thickened and Jub could only see a little way ahead. The shadowy trees looked villainous: tall ghouls with long arms and twiggy fingers. Bushes crouched in the fog as though they were ready to pounce like muggers. Jub hurried on.

"Hello, my small deario."

Jub jumped. A twisted old woman with a face like the bark of a tree and horrible claw hands was standing on the path in front of Jub. She had fierce red eyes like poisonous berries.

"What's in the sack?"

"Let me pass, please," said Jub.

"What's in the sack, I said!"

The old woman had grabbed hold of Jub's arm. Her touch nipped like pepper.

"Let me alone!" gasped Jub. "I must go on."

"Shut up!" said the vicious old woman, and she spat green spittle in Jub's face. Jub was so shocked that she took a step backwards and tripped over a tree-root. Faster than fury, the old woman was on her and had snatched the sack of Happy Endings.

"I'm having this, my six-fingered deario," she snarled. Then she spat at Jub again and hobbled rapidly away into the darkness and the fog. Jub lay there for a long time, terrified that the witch would return.

The fog began to lift and the moon turned the narrow path through the forest to a long silver finger. An owl's hoot questioned sadly. Jub got to her feet. The Happy Endings were lost! She turned and ran back down the path towards her home, scattering bitter tears into the cold black night.

As Jub ran sobbing through the forest, children in their beds were listening to their bedtime stories. But tonight there were to be no Happy Endings. Hansel and Gretel were trapped screaming in the Gingerbread House while the wicked witch made the oven hotter and hotter. Some of the children started to cry.

Cinderella's foot was too big for the glass slipper. Some of the children started to howl. Snow White died when she bit the poisonous apple and she stayed dead for ever. Some of the children started to scream. The Big Bad Wolf gobbled up Little Red Riding Hood and enjoyed every red mouthful. Some of the children had hysterics. On and on the parents of the children read and worse and worse the stories became. Soon the night was filled with the awful sound of frightened or disappointed children weeping and wailing in their beds.

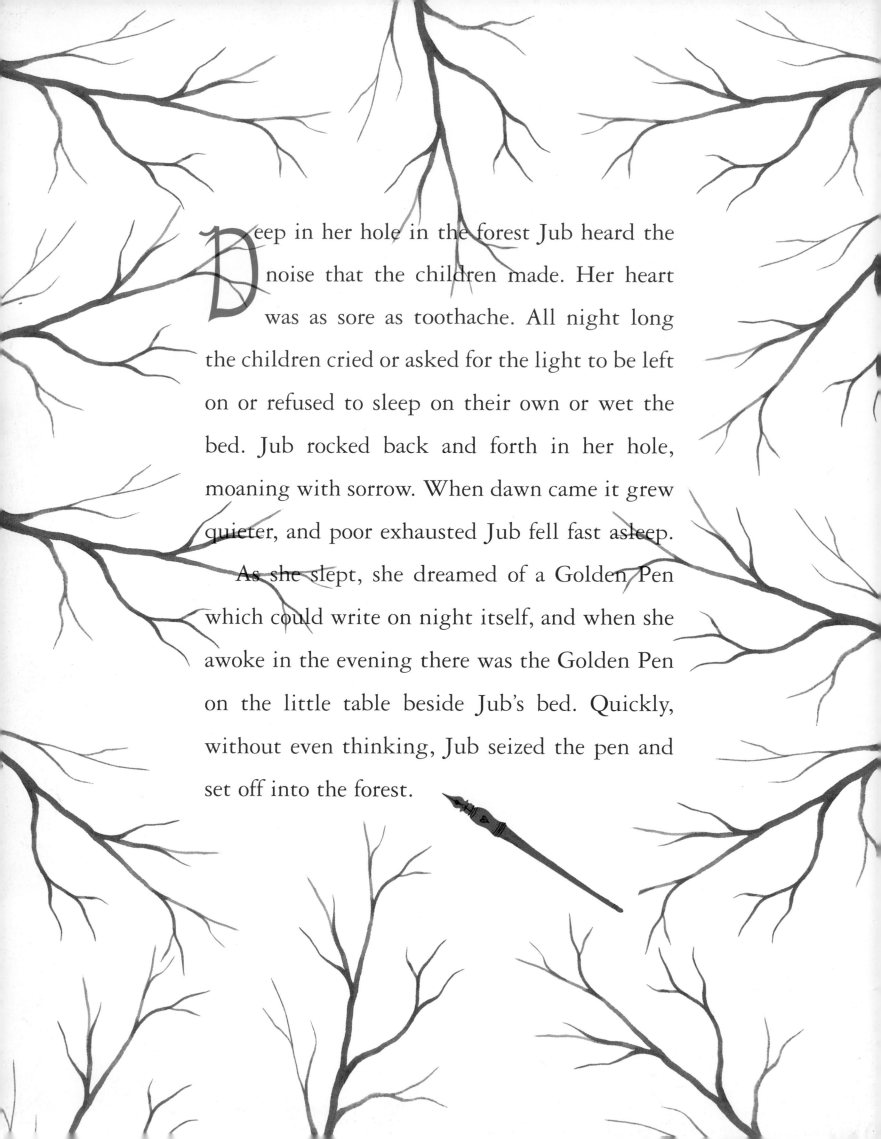

Deep in her hole in the forest Jub heard the noise that the children made. Her heart was as sore as toothache. All night long the children cried or asked for the light to be left on or refused to sleep on their own or wet the bed. Jub rocked back and forth in her hole, moaning with sorrow. When dawn came it grew quieter, and poor exhausted Jub fell fast asleep.

As she slept, she dreamed of a Golden Pen which could write on night itself, and when she awoke in the evening there was the Golden Pen on the little table beside Jub's bed. Quickly, without even thinking, Jub seized the pen and set off into the forest.

It grew dark. The stars whispered to themselves in the black sky. When Jub came near to the spot where the witch had snitched her sack she stopped. She wondered what to do. She held the Golden Pen between her fingers and drew a question mark on the night air. It floated before her, a perfect gold?, glowing in the darkness.

Suddenly Jub knew exactly what to do. She would write her own Happy Ending on the night! She held tightly to the Golden Pen and began. Every word she wrote shone out in perfect golden handwriting …

the witch lived in the

The witch lived in the trunk of a dead tree in the darkest, thorniest part of the forest. When she had first opened the sack of Happy Endings she had been furious. They were worthless to a witch. They were boring and stupid. She had flung the sack into the corner of her lair and gone out again to bite the head off any small bird she could catch and crunch its beak between her long yellow teeth.

But tonight the witch had decided that she was going to burn the sack of Happy Endings to make a fire for herself. She was going to dance around that fire and shout out terrible bad words and then drink poison-berry juice (her favourite tipple) and smoke a clay pipe.

So she lugged the sack outside, added a few dried leaves and twigs, then squatted down and began to rub two sticks together to make a spark to light the fire. Her straggly white hair hung in front of her walnut face as she did so. Before long the rapid movement of her witchy hands had made a spark. Then another. And another. The witch leaned over and, still rubbing, went to start the fire.

As she did so, a spark leapt from the stick and jumped on to a lock of her frizzy old hair. There was a dreadful burny hairy smell, and whumph! The bad old woman's hair was on fire. She shrieked horribly and stood up, beating at her head with her hands. But the flames jumped on to the sleeves of her old black frock and dyed them orange.

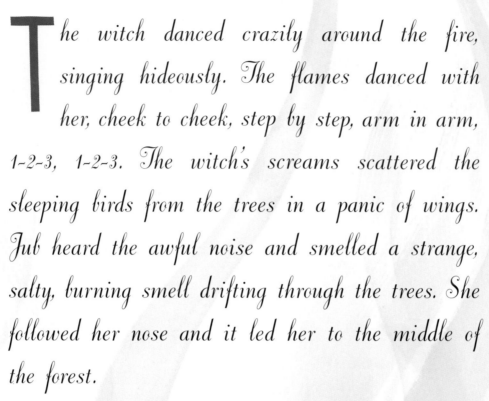

T he witch danced crazily around the fire, singing hideously. The flames danced with her, cheek to cheek, step by step, arm in arm, 1-2-3, 1-2-3. The witch's screams scattered the sleeping birds from the trees in a panic of wings. Jub heard the awful noise and smelled a strange, salty, burning smell drifting through the trees. She followed her nose and it led her to the middle of the forest.

At first she thought she had stumbled upon a fire, spitting and crackling like the breath of a dragon. But then the fire opened its jaws and roared and she saw it was the witch burning to death.

There was nothing Jub could do, even if she had wanted to. She stared in horror into the witch's small red eyes until they were burned completely black and the witch collapsed in a sullen hiss of ash and glowing cinders. The sack of Happy Endings lay on the ground beside her, covered in leaves and twigs but otherwise completely untouched. Jub grabbed the sack and ran as fast as her short legs could carry her towards the huge old oak tree on the other side of the forest ...

When Jub had written the last sentence of her Ending the golden words glowed more brightly than ever against the page of night, then suddenly disappeared. Jub shivered and looked around. She was standing next to the remains of a small fire and holding the sack of Happy Endings in one hand and the Golden Pen in the other. There was a strange chill in the air. But there was still time, if she ran and ran, to send the Happy Endings out into the world for that night's bedtime.

Jub put her sack on her back and turned and ran through the trees as fast as she ever had in her life.

A soft rain began to spit gently on the dull smoky coals of the fire. The moon gaped down at the forest, agog with light. Jub dropped the Golden Pen as she ran, and ran and ran, but I found it in the woods and wrote this with it.